HEIDI HECKELBECK

and the Lost Library Book

By Wanda Coven
Illustrated by Priscilla Burris

LITTLE SIMON

New York London Toronto Sydney New Delhi

LITTLE SIMON
An imprint of Simon & Schuster Children's Publishing Division
1230 Avenue of the Americas, New York, New York 10020
First Little Simon hardcover edition May 2021
Copyright © 2021 by Simon & Schuster, Inc.
Also available in a Little Simon paperback edition.
All rights reserved, including the right of reproduction in whole or in part in any form. LITTLE SIMON is a registered trademark of Simon & Schuster, Inc., and associated colophon is a trademark of Simon & Schuster, Inc. For information about special discounts for bulk purchases, please contact Simon & Schuster Special Sales at 1-866-506-1949 or business@simonandschuster.com.
The Simon & Schuster Speakers Bureau can bring authors to your live event. For more information or to book an event contact the Simon & Schuster Speakers Bureau at 1-866-248-3049 or visit our website at www.simonspeakers.com.
Designed by Ciara Gay
Manufactured in the United States of America 0321 FFG
10 9 8 7 6 5 4 3 2 1
This book has been cataloged with the Library of Congress.
ISBN 978-1-5344-8581-5 (hc)
ISBN 978-1-5344-8580-8 (pbk)
ISBN 978-1-5344-8582-2 (eBook)

CONTENTS

I SPY FUN!

Surprise!

SURPRISE!

Aunt Trudy had a big surprise for Heidi and Henry Heckelbeck. She was taking them to the Brewster Library for the town's Reading Party celebration.

There were going to be authors, illustrators, and more at the party, and Heidi couldn't wait!

"Hop in!" cried Aunt Trudy as she opened the car door.

Both Heidi and Henry scrambled into the back seat and buckled their seat belts.

Heidi laid her shoulder bag on her lap. She liked to take her bag on special outings. It made her feel very grown-up.

Henry had brought a bag too—his spy bag. It had a magnifying glass, a notebook, and a pen inside.

Heidi glared at her brother and said, "Oh no, you're not in SPY mode, are you?"

Henry held up the magnifying glass and winked at his sister.

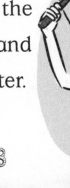

"I'm ALWAYS in spy mode!"

Heidi rolled her eyes.

"Well, I'm in spy mode too!" Aunt Trudy said as she pulled out of the driveway. "And right now, *I spy* your mom waving good-bye."

Aunt Trudy waved at Mom. Henry
did too.

Heidi sighed and looked out the
window. She spied two squirrels
playing tag, but she kept that
information to herself.

She didn't want anyone to know
she was secretly playing.

"I spy a goldendoodle puppy!"
shouted Henry.

Heidi spied the puppy too. It was *so*
cute! But she pretended not to notice.

"I spy a FIRE ENGINE!" cried Henry.

There was a fire engine behind them. Heidi spied her aunt glance at the rearview mirror. Luckily, the sirens were not on, and the fire engine turned down another street.

By now Henry's spy game had kicked into high gear. He spied one thing after another.

"I spy a plane!"

"I spy a cell phone tower!"

"I spy a lady putting on lipstick!"

"I spy two girls eating ice cream!"

Heidi had to cover her ears for the rest of the ride. Finally they turned into the library parking lot, and Heidi smiled.

At least Henry will have to whisper in the library, she thought. *Phew.*

Chapter 2

A SPECIAL CARD

"I spy a parking place!" Henry cried. It was the very last open space.

"Good work!" praised Aunt Trudy, switching on her blinker. "Looks like a big turnout for the Reading Party *and* to sign up for library cards."

Heidi suddenly sat up straight.

"Library cards? May I get one?"

Aunt Trudy patted some papers on the seat beside her. "I brought signed forms so you can *both* get library cards!"

Heidi squealed. "I've always wanted my very own library card!" she said. "I can't wait to put it in my wallet for safekeeping."

"And I'll carry mine in my spy belt," Henry added.

Heidi and Henry raced each other

up the steps to the library. Inside the entrance stood two balloon towers swirled with blue, green, and purple balloons. Heidi and Henry walked past the towers and were greeted by a librarian.

"Good morning!" said the librarian, who wore a silk scarf. "How may I help?"

Henry hopped up and down. "I want to go to the kids' section!" he cried.

The librarian laughed. "I can take you there myself if it's okay with your Aunt Trudy."

Henry looked at his aunt, who nodded.

"That sounds wonderful, Mary," Aunt Trudy said. "Henry, stay in the children's section, and I'll meet you there shortly."

The librarian took Henry by the hand, and off they went.

Heidi turned to her aunt. "Wow! You KNOW the librarian?"

Her aunt winked. "I know *all* the librarians," she said. "I'm a bit of a book wizard."

Heidi checked to see if anyone was listening. Then she whispered, "You're not a wizard! You're a WITCH!"

Aunt Trudy cackled jokingly and linked elbows with Heidi. Together, they skipped over to the line for library cards. After a short wait, it was their turn.

"Hello, Trudy!" said Ms. Egli, the head librarian. "How good to see you! And who have you brought today?"

Heidi was admiring Ms. Egli's necklace. It had an old key hanging from it. Heidi thought it looked magical.

"My name is Heidi," she said with a smile, "and I'm here to get my FIRST library card!"

Aunt Trudy placed the paperwork on the desk, and Ms. Egli entered the information into the computer. Heidi happened to notice a mysterious

smile sweep over
Ms. Egli's face
as she read the
information.
Ms. Egli also
exchanged a
knowing glance
with Aunt Trudy.

Hmm, thought
Heidi. *I wonder what that look was
all about.*

Heidi watched the head librarian
closely. She saw her pull two library
cards from the desk, one for her and
one for her brother.

"It is my pleasure to give you your very first library card," Ms. Egli said, and she handed it to Heidi. The card was black with a gold lion on it.

Then Ms. Egli took the key from around her neck and opened another drawer and pulled out a different card. She smiled at Heidi.

"And now," Ms. Egli went on, "with even greater pleasure, I present you with a second library card . . . a card we only share with very special members of our library community."

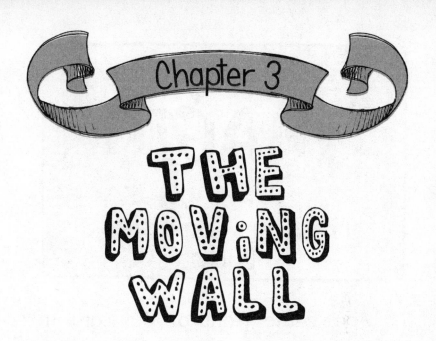

Chapter 3

THE MOVING WALL

Heidi had one word for her special library card: bedazzling.

When she tipped the golden card one way, it shimmered. When she tipped it the other way, rainbow sparkles fluttered from the card and twinkled in the air.

Across the front of the card in glowing letters were the words "Reading is MAGIC." Underneath it read "Brewster's Bewitched Books." Heidi never thought it would be so cool to get a library card.

"Thank you! This is amazing!" said Heidi. "But why did I get two cards?"

"We're not going to the children's section yet," her aunt said. "First I want to share something with you."

Heidi could not imagine what Aunt Trudy had to share at the library—except, of course, for books. And Heidi really loved books.

Aunt Trudy's shoes click-clacked down the long glossy tiled hallway. Heidi picked up her pace to keep up. Her aunt turned left at the water fountain. Then she stopped in front of an oil painting.

It was a portrait of an old librarian dressed like a wizard.

Now it was Aunt Trudy's turn to act like a spy. She looked over both shoulders to make sure they were alone.

"Okay, Heidi. I want you to hold your shimmering library card in front of this painting," her aunt directed.

Heidi raised her eyebrows. "You want me to what?"

Aunt Trudy nudged her forward. "Just give it a try."

Heidi slowly raised her card to the painting. As soon as she did, she heard a *CLUMP* so loud that she jumped at the sound.

The clicking of metal gears became a whirl, and the entire wall with the painting began shaking and then opened. It was a hidden door.

"What is this?" gasped Heidi.

"It's your future!" said her aunt matter-of-factly.

Then Aunt Trudy stepped through the opening and motioned for Heidi to follow.

In a flash, Aunt Trudy was gone! Now it was Heidi's turn. Without thinking twice, she jumped into the opening, and the revolving wall slammed shut behind her.

Chapter 4

THE MAGICAL LIBRARY

"Welcome to the Magical Library!"
Aunt Trudy cheered.

She was waiting on the other side
of the wall.

Heidi's mouth dropped open. "The
MAGICAL Library?"

She could hardly believe her eyes.

Heidi had never seen anything like *this* before.

The bookshelves stretched from the floor to the ceiling. But the ceiling wasn't really a ceiling. It was the night sky, with twinkling stars.

"This is one of the only magical libraries in the world," her aunt told her. "And now you're a member."

Heidi gaped at an enormous

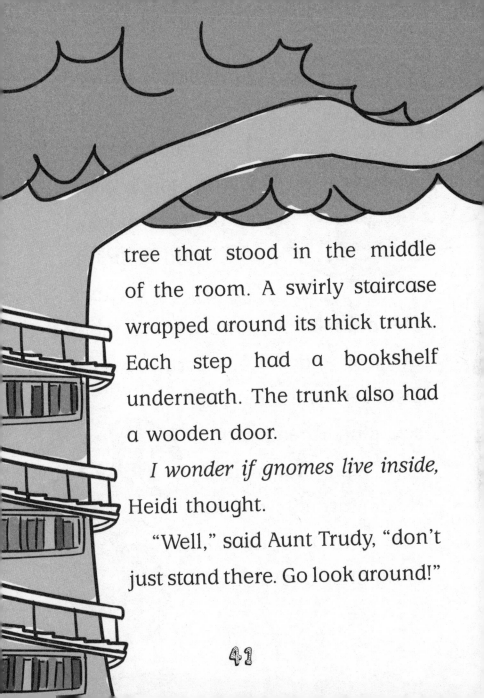

tree that stood in the middle
of the room. A swirly staircase
wrapped around its thick trunk.
Each step had a bookshelf
underneath. The trunk also had
a wooden door.

I wonder if gnomes live inside,
Heidi thought.

"Well," said Aunt Trudy, "don't
just stand there. Go look around!"

Heidi stepped deeper into the library and saw a gigantic globe of the magical world spinning gently on an axis.

She never knew there were so many magical places on earth! In the distance Heidi spied a life-size gingerbread cottage.

In fact, everywhere Heidi turned, she was met with one amazing thing after another.

42

There was a full-scale dragon statue, a swarm of floating books, and a grandfather clock with a door that probably led to another *time* and place. She even saw study desks with feathered quills, and some of the quills were writing all by themselves.

And the entire Magical Library sparkled with tiny white lights.

"Am I dreaming?" Heidi asked.

Aunt Trudy shook her head. "Nope," she said. "This is all real. I've been waiting until you were old enough to bring you here. Brewster has the richest magical history library in the world."

Heidi listened as she watched books magically shelve themselves. Then one book nudged off a shelf and floated across the room toward Heidi. She held out her hands and

caught the book in
her palms.

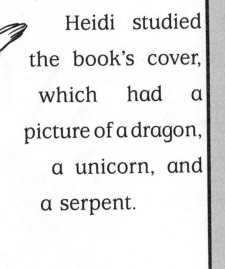

"Wow, do ALL
the books here do
that?" she asked.

"In the Magical Library,
the books often choose *you*
instead of the other way around,"
Aunt Trudy explained.

Heidi studied
the book's cover,
which had a
picture of a dragon,
a unicorn, and
a serpent.

It was called *The History of Magical Creatures*.

"Wow, this looks like MY kind of book!" said Heidi. "May I PLEASE check it out?"

"Of course you can!" Aunt Trudy whispered. "But first we need to find your brother. He's probably collected a stack of books as high as the Empire State Building!"

Heidi didn't want to leave, but she also knew Aunt Trudy was right.

46

Henry loved books . . . sometimes a little too much.

"Okay," Heidi mumbled.

Aunt Trudy put her arm around Heidi. "Don't worry. We can come back here whenever you'd like. But you have to promise me *one* thing."

Heidi nodded and listened closely.

"The Magical Library must remain a secret," Aunt Trudy told her. "Promise you won't tell anyone."

Heidi crossed her heart and said, "I PROMISE."

They left through the secret wall
and found Henry in the children's
section. He was sitting on top of a
pillow, reading a book called *How to
Be a Pirate*. He had a built a wall of
books around himself.

When he saw his family, he waved

and asked, "Can I get ALL these?"

Heidi and Aunt Trudy both laughed.

"You may choose *ten* books to take home," Aunt Trudy said. "But only if you can keep track of *all* of them."

Henry promised he wouldn't lose a single book, but Heidi wasn't so sure.

Chapter 5

FiRST THiNGS FiRST

After the Reading Party, Heidi couldn't wait to dive into *The History of Magical Creatures* the moment she got home. Henry wanted to read his books too.

But it was Sunday, and they had to do their homework and chores first. Heidi got right to work.

For math, she wrote fractions for the missing slices in a pizza. For spelling, she thought of five words that begin with the letter *B*: "bagel," "baby," "bake," "ball," and "banjo."

Then she cleaned her room and emptied the upstairs wastebaskets.

When she finished, Heidi ran downstairs to the kitchen, and Henry raced after her.

"DONE!" she announced to Mom
and Aunt Trudy, who were making
hamburger patties. "May we read our
new library books now?"

Mom washed her hands and dried
them on a towel. Then she pulled out
a bag of chocolate sandwich cookies.

"I have one more task for both of you," she said. "Would you help Aunt Trudy make a peanut butter ice-cream pie for dessert first?"

Heidi and Henry loved ice-cream pie. Maybe the library books could wait a teeny bit longer.

"SURE!" they agreed.

Henry shook the cookies into the food processor. Heidi poured melted butter on top. Then she ground the cookies into crumbs. They took turns patting the cookie crumbs into the pie pan.

After they baked and cooled the crust, Heidi spread peanut butter ice cream on top. She zigzagged chocolate topping over the ice cream. Henry did the same with the peanut butter topping.

Finally, after dinner and dessert, Heidi crawled into bed with her book. She propped up her pillows and flipped through the pages. She began with the history of unicorns.

The mythical and magical unicorn was first discovered in the ancient Lascaux caves in France about fifteen thousand years ago.

Next she read about dragons,

mermaids, yetis, griffins, and some creatures she'd never heard of before, like shimmer fish, rainbow rhinos, dream sprites, and something called a book-eater.

Soon Heidi's eyelids grew heavy. She laid her magical library book on the quilt beside her and fell fast asleep.

In her dreams she rode a unicorn through a meadow of rainbow wildflowers.

Chapter 6

DOODLE DAY

"Heidi!" Mom called. "I thought you were awake. The bus will be here any minute!"

Heidi leaped out of bed, brushed her teeth, and got dressed. Then she raced downstairs. Mom had her backpack and granola bar ready.

Heidi grabbed them and flew out the door.

She ran all the way to the bus and plopped onto the seat beside her brother.

"The bus driver waited JUST for you," Henry said.

"Thank goodness!" said Heidi.

As she started to catch her breath, Heidi realized she had forgotten her *History of Magical Creatures* book at home.

Oh rats! I could have read it during free time, she thought. If Heidi had it her way, she would've read her new library book all day long.

The school day dragged. In math, nobody seemed to understand fractions. Mrs. Welli had to explain *everything*. Heidi got bored and pulled out her notebook and doodled a dragon—just like the one from her book.

During reading, the class took turns reading out loud. The story was about two pigs who were best friends. Heidi doodled a pig with wings in her notebook. She pretty much doodled magical animals all day long. She even made a yeti in art with a paper plate and some cotton balls.

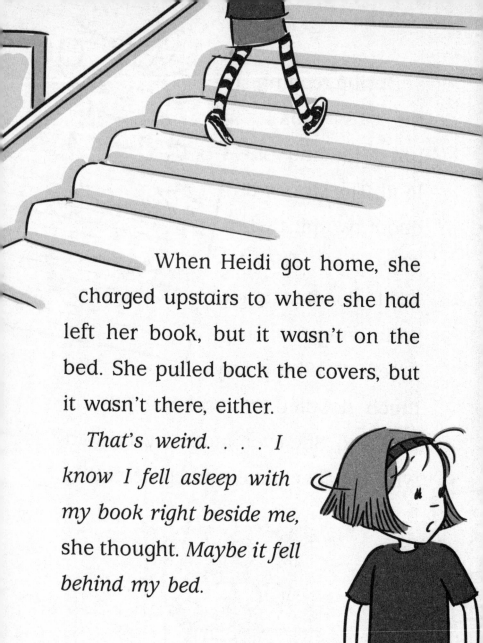

When Heidi got home, she charged upstairs to where she had left her book, but it wasn't on the bed. She pulled back the covers, but it wasn't there, either.

That's weird. . . . I know I fell asleep with my book right beside me, she thought. *Maybe it fell behind my bed.*

Heidi got on her hands and knees
to peer under the bed. The book
wasn't there. Next she searched her
entire room, but *The History of Magical
Creatures* was nowhere to be found.

There was only one last place to look. Heidi had a good idea where her book had gone.

She marched into brother's room and said, "The joke's over, Henry. Give me back my book."

Henry was sitting on his floor reading. He looked at his sister. "I didn't take it. I've already got too many of my OWN books to read."

Heidi stormed out of Henry's room and went downstairs to Mom's office.

"Have you seen my library book?"
she asked.

Mom looked up from her desk.
"No, Heidi. I've been working *all* day."

"Hmm," said Heidi. "Do you think
Dad has it?"

Mom gave Heidi a silly look. "Now,
why would Dad take your library
book?"

"I don't know, but it's gone," said Heidi. "And it couldn't have walked away by itself."

This made her mom laugh. "Well, I can help you look after I finish this report."

"It's okay," said Heidi. "I'll just have to look a little harder."

Chapter 7

BOOKNAPPERS!

"My book is not lost!" Heidi declared as she climbed down from the tree house.

She was on an all-out search. She checked the tree house. She checked the bushes. She checked Mom's and Dad's cars.

Then she went back to her room, stripped the quilt off her bed, and shook it. She flapped her blankets this way and that. She even yanked the sheets off her bed. But there was no sign of her book.

Still, Heidi didn't give up. She
checked behind her nightstand, her
dresser, and her desk, and she looked
all through her closet. But the book
was nowhere to be found.

What if I really DID lose my library book? she wondered. *Will I have to pay a fine? Will I be allowed to practice magic anymore?! Will I go to WITCH DETENTION?*

As Heidi's imagination ran wild, she noticed something else missing from her bookshelves.

"My books!" she cried. "They're all GONE!"

Heidi ran to her bookshelves and patted the empty spaces. Then she heard a strange flutter above her head.

She was about to look up when her mother called from downstairs. "HEIDI! I need HELP!"

Heidi walked down to the kitchen and found Mom searching through the cabinets.

"What's up?" Heidi asked.

"It's my cookbook," Mom declared. "I left it *right* here in the bookstand to make dinner, but it's disappeared!"

Heidi's eyes grew wide. "That's weird," she said. "I'm missing books too!"

Then Dad burst into the kitchen from the basement. "Big trouble, everyone! My secret soda notebook is gone," he cried.

Heidi and Mom exchanged a glance, but before they could say anything, there was a heart-stopping scream from upstairs.

Mom, Dad, and Heidi raced to Henry's room to see what was the matter.

Henry stood in a pile of toys, clothes, and trash from an overturned wastebasket.

"My library books are MISSING," he told them.

Mom put her hand over her heart. "Is that *all*?" she said. "You scared us."

Henry stared at his mother helplessly. "But you don't understand. I lost ALL TEN books! Aunt Trudy is never going to take me to the library again!"

Mom and Dad both shook their heads.

"They must be here somewhere," Dad said. "Let's see if we can help you find them."

"And let's tidy up while we're at it," Mom added.

Heidi watched her family as they began to clean her brother's room. For one thing, Mom and Dad *never* helped her clean *her* room.

And for another thing, something really *weird* was going on. How could the *whole* family be missing books at the *same time*?

Then a funny feeling swept over Heidi.

This must be MAGIC, she thought. *And I have a hunch who—or what— might be stealing our books.*

Chapter 8

BiPPiTY! BOPPiTY! BOODLEY-BAR!

Heidi ran to her room and pulled out her doodle notebook. She flipped through her doodles of magical creatures and found a picture she had drawn of a flying book. Underneath it she had written the name "book-eater."

The History of Magical Creatures
had explained that book-eaters were
invisible creatures that loved stories
and gobbled up books.

"Oh no," gasped Heidi. "I thought 'gobble up' meant they read books, but what if book-eaters actually EAT books?! I've got to stop this right away!"

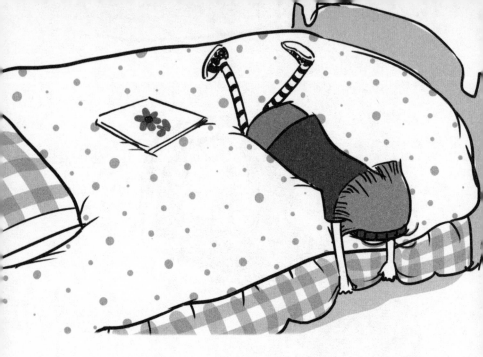

But how could she find a book-eater? They were invisible, after all, unless they chose to show themselves.

Hmm, if magic is the problem, Heidi thought, *maybe magic is the answer, too. I'll grab my . . . Uh-oh.* Suddenly she was struck with a horrible thought:

What if the book-eater ate my Book of Spells*?!*

Heidi ran to her bed, pulled up the dust ruffle, and peered underneath. Her spell book was still there. She grabbed the book and hugged it like a long-lost friend. Then she searched for a spell that would allow her to *see* the book-eater.

Come out! Come out! Wherever You Are!

Do you have a mouse in your house? Or perhaps you have a chipmunk hiding behind your washing machine? Or could it be you have an invisible creature in your midst? If you need a critter to show its rascally little face, then this is the spell for YOU!

Ingredients:

1 bottle of honey

1 handful of rainbow sprinkles

1 bath towel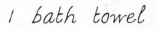

1 object the creature desires most

Lay the bath towel on the floor. Place the object on the towel. Squeeze a circle of honey around the object. Scatter rainbow sprinkles on top. Then hold your medallion in one hand, and place your other hand on top of the object. Chant the following spell:

BiPPiTY! BoPPiTY! BooDLeY-BaR!

CoMe OuT! CoMe OuT!

WHeReVeR, YoU aRe!

Heidi collected all the ingredients and laid the towel on the floor. She placed her *Book of Spells* on the towel and squeezed a circle of honey around it. Then she scattered the rainbow sprinkles on top. She grabbed her medallion and cast the spell.

Poof!

A cloud of mist rose from the spell circle. Heidi couldn't see one single thing!

Chapter 9

THE BOOK THiEF

Heidi waved the mist away and gasped. A creature stood before her. He was about three feet tall, with large round blue eyes and a pointy nose. His ears stuck out of his head on two short fuzzy stems, and the tops flopped over like puppy ears.

It was the book-eater.

The creature reached for the *Book of Spells*, but something pushed his hand back. Heidi realized her spell had created a magical force field around her book.

"That's one book you CANNOT have," Heidi said fiercely.

The book-eater pulled his hands close to his body.

Heidi frowned. "What do you think you're doing?"

"I want that book!" the book-eater confessed. "Magic books make me feel most at home. They have yummy words and old pages that smell like dust and knowledge. And this place is not like my home."

Heidi folded her arms. "That's because this is MY home," she said. "And you can't keep stealing our books."

The book-eater suddenly looked very sad. "I miss my home," he said.

Heidi's face lit up as she had a new idea that could solve everyone's problems. "Maybe I can help you get back home," she suggested. "What exactly does YOUR home look like?"

The book-eater held his arms wide. "My home is big and full of magical books, and it's the most wonderful place ever! Oh, I miss it ever so much."

Heidi clapped her hands. "Aha! You must live in the Magical Library!" she said. "But how did you end up here?"

The book-eater pulled *The History of Magical Creatures* out of thin air.

"My library book!" Heidi yelped.

The book-eater nodded. "I was napping inside it. When I woke up, I was here."

Heidi held out her hand, and the book-eater handed her the library book. She hugged it in the same way she had hugged her *Book of Spells*.

"How did you get INSIDE this book?"

The book-eater showed Heidi how he got into books. He pulled a book of fairy tales—*one of Heidi's*—from his backpack and opened it. Then *swoosh*! He jumped in the pages and disappeared. Then *swish*! He jumped back out.

"Book-eaters are made to live inside books!" he said with a little smile.

Heidi was beginning to like the little book thief. He didn't seem like such a bad creature after all. She decided to properly introduce herself.

"By the way, my name is Heidi."

The book-eater smiled wider. "My name is Inkspot, but my friends call me Inkster."

Heidi set down her library book. "Well, it's nice to meet you, Inkster. Maybe we can help each other. If you return my family's books, then I'll take you back to the Magical Library."

Inkster's eyes brightened. "*Really?* I'd like that *very* much."

Then Heidi and Inkster shook on it.

Chapter 10

BOOK RETURN

Inkster was only visible to Heidi—thanks to his magic. The book-eater was used to being invisible, and he liked it that way.

"I'll check on my family while you put my books back," she said.

Inkster agreed with a nod.

Heidi tiptoed across the hall and peeked into Henry's room. Mom, Dad, and Henry were still busy looking for the lost books.

"The coast is clear," Heidi told her new friend.

Inkster quickly threw Heidi's books into the air, and they flew back to her shelves.

Then Inkster floated
downstairs   to   place
Mom's   cookbook   on
the   bookstand   and
return Dad's secret soda
notebook to his basement laboratory.

"What   about   Henry's   books?"
Heidi whispered when the book-eater
came back. "How can we return them

without him knowing?"

Inkster gave a little
snicker. "Oh, they
won't   be   able   to
see me at all if you
distract them."

Heidi gave him a thumbs-up. "Okay, but be careful!"

She took a deep breath and walked casually into Henry's room. "So, did you find your books yet?" asked Heidi as if she didn't know.

Henry shook his head sadly. "I found this hard gum that was stuck under my bed, but not one book!"

"Ew," said Heidi. "Well, maybe I can help! I mean, I just found Mom and Dad's lost books downstairs."

"You did?" Heidi's parents said at the same time. Then they both gave her a hug.

"Yuck!" cried Henry as he closed his eyes. "This is a no-hugging-sisters area!"

Now! thought Heidi, and Inkster darted into the room and left Henry's books behind his desk.

"Okay, okay," said Mom as she let go of Heidi. "I always forget about your no-hugging rule, Henry."

Heidi used the moment to wander over to Henry's desk. "Um, are these your books behind the desk?"

Henry ran over and counted his books. "I can't believe it! They are ALL here!"

Then Henry gave his sister the biggest hug.

"What about your rule, Henry?" asked Dad.

"Some rules are made to be broken," he said, and everyone laughed.

Whales

by Heidi Heckelbeck

The rest of the week went by fast. Heidi left lots of books for Inkster while she was at school, and Inkster even helped her finish a book report about whales.

Finally, on Saturday, Heidi, Aunt Trudy, and Inkster returned to the Magical Library.

"Thanks for bringing me home," said Inkster. "Now . . . do you want to see the most secret parts of the library?"

Heidi smiled slyly. "I thought you'd never ask!"

Check out the next book starring

Ker-plunk! Mom dropped a box labeled HEIDI WINTER on the kitchen counter.

Ker-thunk! Dad dropped another box beside it, labeled HENRY WINTER.

Heidi was the first one to spy the box with her name on it. "What's in THERE?" she asked.

An excerpt from *Heidi Heckelbeck and the Snow Day Surprise*

Henry looked over and spotted the box with *his* name on it. "Let me guess," he said. "Is THAT where we're going to LIVE this winter?"

Heidi rolled her eyes. "Do you really think we're going to hibernate in boxes, like bears in a cave?!"

Henry held up his hands. "Well, why not? We can each have our own PRIVATE space, finally!"

Mom laughed and opened Heidi's box. She pulled out a snowflake sweater. "These boxes have winter clothes to keep you two bear cubs warm," she explained.

An excerpt from *Heidi Heckelbeck and the Snow Day Surprise*

Dad opened Henry's box and said, "We got them out of storage because we heard it might snow today!"

Heidi and Henry looked at each other and squealed.

"Does that mean we're going to have a SNOW day?" asked Heidi.

Dad switched on the TV. "Let's listen to the weather report and find out!" he said.

Heidi and Henry sat at the breakfast table and faced the TV.

"There's Melanie Maplethorpe's MOM!" cried Heidi, pointing at the TV.

An excerpt from *Heidi Heckelbeck and the Snow Day Surprise*